Mayor

Mrs Gobbledegook

s book belongs to:

B

Pete

Me

Baker

For Imogen

S.C.

For Boris and Milan

D.D.

First published in 2011
by Meadowside Children's Books
185 Fleet Street, London EC4A 2HS
www.meadowsidebooks.com

Text © Susan Chandler
Illustrations © Delphine Durand
The rights of Susan Chandler and Delphine Durand
to be identified as the author and illustrator of this
work have been asserted by them in accordance with
the Copyright, Designs and Patents Act, 1988

A CIP catalogue record for this book
is available from the British Library
1 2 3 4 5 6 7 8 9 10

Printed in China

Welcome to Cuckooville

Written by
Susan Chandler
and illustrated by
Delphine Durand

meadowside 🍃
CHILDREN'S BOOKS

In the middle of Cuckooville there was a clock. A cuckoo clock. But behind the doors of the cuckoo clock there was... well... nothing. **Not a cuckoo in sight!**

Instead, every hour, one of the townsfolk would run up the steps and burst through the little wooden doors, shouting out the time. How they loved being the cuckoo, **especially**...

...Mrs Gobbledygook.

'**Lumpyplums snufflybapz!**'

she sang from the top of the clock.

The Mayor stopped and shook his head.
'Right! From now on, everyone takes their turn
at being the cuckoo, everyone except you,
Mrs Gobbledygook. We don't need to know
about your snuffly plums, thank you!

We need to know the time!'

'Actually, it was
lumpyplums,'
added a little boy called Pete.
(Who was quite clever.)

Poor Mrs Gobbledygook. No one in the town could understand her.

'Dropsy bubbly?'

asked the Grocer.

'Squishy warts?'

queried the Baker.

'What's an Oobie noobie, when it's at home?' questioned the Butcher.

If only she could prove to the rest of
Cuckooville that speaking Gobbledygook
could be useful. Then she could take
her turn at being the cuckoo again.

One day, a strange vehicle came rumbling over the hills. The townsfolk stood and stared.

'Where did they come from?' the Baker quivered.

'Who are they?' the Grocer wobbled.

'I haven't got enough sausages!' the Butcher shuddered.

'What do they want?' the Mayor whimpered, starting to panic.

The vehicle stopped.
The doors opened.
The steps came down.

'Visitors!'
cried the Grocer,
tossing some
tomatoes.

'Strangers!' yelped the Baker, lobbing buns in the air.

'Aliens!' boomed the Butcher, chucking his chops in a fluster.

The townsfolk panicked and ran in all directions until...

...they got tangled together
and landed in a hysterical heap!

The stranger spoke.
The townsfolk wriggled.
The Mayor popped out.

'Hum
honky
nubs,'
the stranger
said.

'W-w-what!?'
stuttered
the Mayor.

'He sounds like
Mrs Gobbledygook,'
Pete piped up.

But no one seemed
to hear him.

But just then, Mrs Gobbledygook appeared! She marched right past the Mayor and greeted the strangers with a smile. **'Nubbly crubs!'** she said politely.

'Nubbly crubs!' said the strangers.

'Fluffy snops egg dropsy wink,' pointed Mrs Gobbledygook.

'She's telling
them to get lost!'
hissed the Grocer.

'She's giving
them what for!'
barked the Baker.

'She wants a
big sloppy kiss,'
whispered the
Butcher.

'She's giving
them directions!'
said Pete loudly.

'Ahh!'

'Ahh!' breathed the towns folk with relief. 'Directions!'

'Ahh!'

'Directions!'
said the Mayor, realising that all the panic had been for nothing. Actually, he felt a little embarrassed.

Then he turned to Mrs Gobbledygook and whispered something.

Mrs Gobbledygook nodded her head and then walked towards the clock...

'Bobbledy
plop
Cuckooville!'

Mrs Gobbledygook
shouted from the top
of the clock.

'Which means,' said the Mayor,

'Welcome to Cuckooville!'

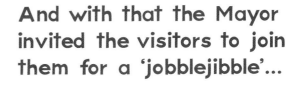

And with that the Mayor invited the visitors to join them for a 'jobblejibble'...

...which to you and me
is, of course,
a party!

You are now leaving

Cuckooville

Twinned with Wobbleton Gobblesville